An Urban Fantasy Sherlock Holmes Mystery

SPECTOR

John Pirillo

Copyright 2022

GRAVEYARD

He can see the lights are on inside the Abbey. Smiles and hefts a tiny box with intricate wiring twisted about its top. He grips it tightly, "Soon, old friend. Soon."

Another man, standing in the shadows net to him asks, "You are sure this will work?"

He twists about and holds the box towards the other man. Briefly light catches the side of his face as he turns, revealing a scar beneath the right ear. "Would you like to test the device?"

The device began to throw sparks from the coils of wire and light up in his hand.

The other man at once holds up his hands in denial. "Rather not."

He smiles at the other man's fear, nods. "Wise decision." He dials down the device, then returns his attention to the abbey. "You sure he will go to his office as usual?"

"He is like a family clock. Never misses a tick, or a tock."

"Good. Once you have entered, I will hand over the device. Make sure you have your own task ready at hand as well."

The other man nodded. He patted his right coat pocket. "Right here."

THE ABBEY

Archbishop O'Reilly clucked to himself like a hen as he replaced spent candle sticks, reduced to no more than melted stumps, on the silver trays of the altar. The fresh candles were fragrant, even before being lit. They made his nostrils tickle.

Happily, he finished the trade of old with new, then once finished, he reached under the marble stand the candles sat upon, where he kept a box of wooden matches hidden.

He pulled out the box, then opened it, and removed a match. Then he struck the rough side of the box with the math. An explosion of light greeted and dazzled his vision for a moment, sending splashes of light, then shadow about him. Shivers of yellow sparks and flame danced with the darkness. He carefully lit each of the new candles in a ceremonial way he had fallen into by habit over the years.

Right left. Left right. Right left. Left right, and each time marching forward with his match to light the next row of wicks.

The candles were special.

He had used what little money he had, to import them

from France. They were holy candles, prayed over while carved.

While he felt nothing especially overwhelming about their looks, just the idea of it was enough to make up for their drabber appearance than the ones he replaced.

Flames from the newly lit candles did, however, exude a gentle fragrance like sandalwood, which he found soothing and refreshing at the same time. And the wicks burned brightly, sending curling yellow and gold flames upwards towards the ceiling.

He used only the best and most Holy items in his abbey. And these candles were quite special, as well as holy. Made from a wax blessed by Holy Mother Frances of Paris, who could chase a vampire away with one word, stop a werewolf in its tracks with a wave of her fingers, and raise a chorus of angels with a simple prayer.

Yes, blessed to have these treasures, indeed. And now, his church as well.

"Come, Henry," Archbishop O'Reilly said to his assistant. "We are finished preparing for the morrow. You may take the remaining candles and store them in the Quiet Room. Their fragrance will help any who pray there."

"Yes, Archbishop!" Henry, his loyal assistant, replied. "At once."

"Wait!"

Henry turned to view Archbishop O'Reilly's face. "Sir?"

"Make sure the box is placed on the bottom shelf near the door, so they don't melt from the heat of the day when the sunlight strikes through the stained-glass windows."

"Yes, sir!"

Henry turns to leave again.

"And…"

Henry turns back.

Archbishop O'Reilly smiles benevolently upon his young assistant. "They're blessed and we are blessed having them here."

Henry nodded, eager smile gracing his young lips. The archbishop was quite fussy, but kind. His assistant, a young man with a freckled face and straw yellow hair smiled and nodded. "Thank you, Archbishop. Shall endeavor my best to do so immediately."

But this was not Henry's lucky day, there was more. There was always more with the archbishop. *God bless him.*

"Come, come now, Henry, you know I do not like being so formal. It is for the children who attend prayers, not my friends. Children need someone to look up to."

The archbishop grinned at Henry. "My friends do not."

He smiled and as Henry shifted the candles, its weight growing more ponderous the longer he was detained, the archbishop put a friendly hand on Henry's right shoulder. "Please call me O'Reilly. I may speak English, but I am Irish all the way through and through."

O'Reilly did a cute dance step a couple of moments before his surprised assistant. "See. Me feet move like a leprechaun's too."

Henry laughed, then gave the archbishop a surprised look. "You've never told me your name before."

"Oh, but I have. Just have not pointed it out loudly enough when you were listening to me. But then, that may be...the archbishop winked at Henry...because most times your mind is on Natalie, is it not?"

Henry blushed.

The archbishop grinned. "Do not worry I will not let anyone else know I am onto you, not even your fair Natalie's father. Know he can be kind of brutish at times."

Henry bursts into laughter. "I will be betting not a one of your followers are aware of that. He puts on a good s how in public."

Archbishop O'Reilly smiled. "It is our little secret. Now get along. You are young and need your rest."

He gave Henry a wink. "After you've secretly met with Natalie of course."

Henry blushed even deeper than last time. Smiled.

"But you're older, don't you need sleep too?"

"Time enough to rest when the Lord calls on me to come home to Him."

Henry begins to tear up. His voice catches as he says, "I pray that never happens."

Archbishop O'Reilly hugs Henry to him. "There, there child. Death is not our enemy. He is the gatekeeper to the finest of homes ever...with our Lord."

Archbishop O'Reilly lets go of Henry. "Now, shelf the candles and hurry home, we don't want your good mother to worry over you being out late at night, do we?"

"No, sir."

"Good!"

Archbishop O'Reilly turns away from Henry and heads for the door leading to his office. He turns back. Henry is watching him. His face is so sweet and kind that it makes Archbishop O'Reilly wish that he had become a real father instead of one of the Church.

Then he shuts the door into his office as he enters.

Henry sighs and begins working his way towards the front doors of the abbey where the Quiet Room is. He freezes at the sound of an ear-piercing scream.
The archbishop's scream.

" Archbishop O'Reilly!" Henry shouts, dropping the box of candles as he turns to run for the archbishop's office door.

He slams it open.

Inside, Archbishop O'Reilly lays across his large wooden desk, eyes staring at the ceiling overhead, hands crossed over his chest, as if peacefully resting. But his face filled with horror.

A huge slash is in Archbishop O'Reilly gown, but there is no sign of blood.

Or of a knife.

Or of a killer.

Then blood begins to flow from the slash.

And flow.

And flow.

And…

Except, the color of the blood is all wrong!

GHOST IN THE NIGHT

Henrietta Storm woke up with a start. Her delicate shoulders wet with clumps of sticky sweat, even though all she had over her was a light nightgown.

After all, it was summer, and one just didn't wear heavy night gowns to bed when the temperatures were high and uncomfortable.

Henrietta was a conservative woman and believed in using energy wisely as the power company often reminded. "Lights off, so lights don't have to stay off."

As if Edison and Tesla's electric power supplies would ever run out. Jules Verne and Herbert Wells had helped the two older men to construct a version of the engine which powered the Master of the World, their fabulous flying vehicle. The device used...she frowned to remember what they called the power source. Ah! She remembered.

"Strings." She laughed. *Who could ever have imagined a power supply that used strings?*

So, she laughed at the concept of running out of power. The elders who ran the power plant were still in the habit of thinking it was the old steam-powered systems, run by coal and wood. No wonder they worried over the power running out. But few were still using steam-powered anything anymore, and still fewer yet, electricity derived from the old fuels. Especially once Jules and Wells discovered that coal was polluting the air and environment.

Sure, Henrietta found it amusing, that old slogan, but the newer one was even more ridiculous. "Be cool, but not too."

She rubbed at her eyes. Sleep was refusing to let go of the waking realm. She blinked her eyes. Several times to wash the sleep from them, and the dream that had disturbed her so much once she awakened. Yet, which she still seemed to be partly stuck in.

It was unusual...in that it seemed to cling to her like the fog in the early morning would to her bare ankles. Or the silk of a spider web against your face when you walked into one.

She let out a gasp when she saw that part of her dream was now intruding into her bedroom. Standing in the right corner of her bedroom, on an invisible table. Invisible, to our world surely, but to her dream world, it was there, even though it did not belong. No dining table ever belongs in a comfortable bedroom, especially when that table is filled with fresh cooked food and the sounds of friendly chatter.

But even though friendly, the oddness of it all had awoken her still further. It was like a nightmare, yet unlike any before.

"I must still be dreaming," she chided herself, and sat back on her bed to slide under the sheet once more. But then something bright moved into view to her left.

She sat back up, startled.

A Spector stood at the closest end of the table to her bed. Next to an invisible table, which was somehow visible, and casting a moonlight bright glow about the room.

Suddenly, the dream, nightmare, became too real. Too much to shuffle off as a bad dream.

She felt sweat on her shoulders turn into freezing cold fear.

Henrietta did the only reasonable thing a frightened person might do at such an uncanny moment. Especially, when the Spector turned about to stare at her, its eyes very human, but its skin as bright and white as a full moon.

"Hello, Henrietta," the Spector greeted her with an empty smile. "It's so nice to finally meet you."

Henrietta screamed!

Holmes shook his head repeatedly. "I do not believe in ghosts, John. Sorry."

Doctor Watson shook his head, just as stubbornly fixed in his belief that there were ghostly things, even as Holmes was plainly a non-believer and not the least bit interested in what he considered as fancy ideas with no scientific basis.

Watson his head vigorously. "Well, I saw one!"

"And you have as well in the past.'

Holmes paused a moment in his reading to look up at Watson. "True. But ghosts do not harm people. They are merely enhanced, ethereal manifestations of the soul. Souls locked onto our plane of existence because of fear, or trauma. They are visible only because they are drawing upon our own fear to materialize them. And as such they have no more power than that which we give them."

"But" Watson began.

"But" Holmes continued, pointing his pipe at Watson like a lecturer at school, "My dear Watson, to believe that a ghost, or disembodied human, can cause the death of another...such as us, is impossible for me to accept. Yes, they could, in theory, edge a person on through their fear to do something they might otherwise have never considered. Perhaps, they could even in extreme cases…but rarely…possess a living person who were so violently negative that they opened the door of their aura, to their body so another soul could enter then perhaps."

"Perhaps what, Holmes?"

"Perhaps they could then…not at once mind you, but over an extended period of time began to influence one's thinking to the point of it deteriorating one's moral convictions."

"Then?"

"They yes, perhaps they might hurt someone, but only by using a mortal body."

"Well then, how do you explain the unusual sightings of late?"

"I don't," Holmes replied calmly. "Yet." He put his pipe back into his mouth, folded the early morning edition of the London Times into his lap, then continued. "I rather fancy there are ghosts, Watson, I just don't believe they would deliberately go out night after night and slit a man or woman's throat. Just for the pleasure of it."

"Like the Ripper did."

Holmes eyed Watson carefully. "You believe the Ripper is back. After all these years, after all we did to put a stop to that hideous creature."

Watson snorted. "Maybe. Maybe, not. But you cannot rule out the fact that this ghost has been seen repeatedly by reliable witnesses."

"Ghosts have no substance to see."

"Well, this one most certainly has."

Homes templed his fingers against his chin and thought a moment. "John, have you ever read about the *Spector* of McCumberly Castle?"

Watson, surprised at both the use of his first name and of that of the castle, was shocked for a moment. "Touché, Holmes. Now I am shocked as well." Watson pondered his next words a long time then admitted, "Maybe I have."

Then quickly, "Perhaps I have, but it still doesn't explain what's been happening throughout London."

Then added further, "Or who has seen this mysterious Spector!"

Holmes smiled. He loved John, but the man could be as

stubborn as a mountain to move, or a bulldog with its teeth locked on the back of your pants once he set his mind on something.

"What? Two drunks and a sleep-deprived bus driver?"

Holmes chuckled, which turned Watson livid with ager for a moment, then he sighed deeply. The two of them cared too dearly for each other to stay mad for long at one another.

'Granted, not the most reliable sources."

Holmes chuckled again. "The first two probably couldn't see their own forefingers or thumb, and the last was lucky he didn't kill himself and his passengers in a bus accident."

Holmes continued. "The man should not have been looking down a dark alley for Midnight Angels, when he should have been driving straight along the road."

Holmes shook his head. "No wonder he lied to save his job...and his reputation."

"And you know that how?"

Holmes stared Watson in the eyes. "The accident happened where, Watson?"

"Halfway Street. Why?"

"Halfway Street is known to have five or six of the young, lovely Midnight Angels in all its alleys at night and Inspector Bloodstone spoke with me last night about a certain bus driver who had been warned about not drinking

on the job."

Holmes chuckled. "The one who had the accident."

Watson finally let sighed. "Well, I suppose you could be right about those three then."

Ms. Hudson, who has been seated at the windows, knitting her favorite design, baby pants for a young boy, finally stopped knitting. Finally, unable to remain silent, she looked up from her knitting. "John, Holmes is not being overly dramatic or stubbornly fussy about this. You are being a grumbly bear again. You are. Holmes, like the charming man he is, and the kind friend he is, is merely being polite."

Watson gave her a startled look. "Grumbly bear! Really?"

Both Holmes and Ms. Hudson broke into laughter.

Watson blushed with embarrassment.

Ms. Hudson set her knitting down and came to Watson at the sitting room table and wrapped her arms about his neck and hugged him. "My dear, dear beloved Watson, this time of day is the only part in which he can stop sleuthing and find some moments of peace before work begins once anew once more. While you, my love, blather on and on about ghosts, like that rascally Challenger does at times, when he is too stubborn to let go of his viewpoint."

"My dear, I have never heard you go on so extremely like this."

Holmes pointed his pipe again at Watson." Beware the viper who rests silently at your feet, lest he strike when you least expect it."

Ms. Hudson laughed. "Why thank you, Holmes. I rather thought of myself as a she bears trying to soothe her grumbly bear's feelings."

Watson gave her an alarmed look. "I am so sorry, my dear." He turned to Holmes. "You have been quite kind...as usual...to hear me rant and rave and go on about it I'm starting to sound more like Conan than myself."

Ms. Hudson gave Watson another hug and returned to retrieve her knitting. "Yes, but Conan, bless his heart, is merely trying to inform us of his theories."

Holmes nodded. "And oftentimes they are quite correct, or at least on the right track. After all, he and Harry have broken up quite a few of those prank mediums lately."

"Ah, that explains why they are not here this morning as usual," Watson spoke.

Ms. Hudson returned to her knitting and finishing a cute baby bear head on the pants front, which could be unclasped for a young boy to go to the bathroom. "John, I love both you and Conan. But he has a calling to expose fake mediums. You do not. And especially ghosts which do not exist."

Holmes eyed Ms. Hudson. She blushed. "Well, for the most part they do not."

Homes grinned.

Watson smiled. "Pray that side of me is never aroused. Or like a mad jinn aroused angrily from its centuries old sleep in a cramped old wine bottle, I shall be quite the intolerable soul."

Holmes chuckled. "I am sure Conan would not like that anymore than you. He is rather disposed to believing he is the only one who is out to expose the fake mediums, when in fact, Harry and I have been doing it quietly for years now."

Ms. Hudson smiled. "And I am so lucky to have so many good friends who care so much about each other and the world."

"And like all good friends, we poke at our weak spots from time to time," Watson agreed amiably.

"Ouch!" Holmes teased.

Watson barked with laughter, then rose from the sitting room table and went to the windows overlooking Baker Street. "Who would have ever thought we would live to see such modern times, Holmes. "

Holmes went back to browsing the London Times, then froze. "Watson, I need you to do me a favor at once."

"What is it?"

"Want you to carry a message to Inspector Bloodstone."

Watson gave Holmes a puzzled look.

Holmes folded the London Times once more, but this time he rose from his chair by the fire, allowing his lap blanket to slide to the floor. "The game's afoot!"

"Isn't it always?" Watson asked, not expecting a reply with any kind of immediate explanation. Holmes rarely explained in advance when he was onto something big or relevant.

Holmes gave John a sudden grin. "Why? Did you have a date planned with Ms. Hudson?"

Ms. Hudson giggled. Watson glared at her a moment, then cracked a smile. "It was sort of on my...ummm...mind."

Ms. Hudson's eyes widened a moment, then she blushed.

Holmes swept from the room to the staircase, flinging on his cape and cap as he passed the coat hanger by the staircase.

It made a rattling sound as it rocked back and forth, tapping the wall after Holmes had jerked his clothing from it.

Watson hurriedly grabbed his own coat and hat and hurried after Holmes.

The coat rack almost fell over in his urgency.

Ms. Hudson spotted it and rushed to catch it.

Watson came back inside and gave her a peck. "Sorry, thanks!"

He started out again, then glanced back at Ms. Hudson. "Maybe tomorrow?"

Ms. Hudson giggled and pushed him back towards the stairs.

She turned around and clutched at her heart, sighed happily, then returned to pick up her knitting and work on the pants for the young boy.

The one she hoped she and Watson would one day have.

BAKER STREET

Holmes paused to get into an electric taxi, while Watson waited for his to arrive. "Watson, let the Inspector know we will be busy for the rest of this day and please do hurry, as the Queen wants to speak with both of us."

Watson's eyebrows rose. "The Queen. But Holmes, how could she possibly be expecting us? She does not even know we are coming?"

"Indeed!" Holmes replied, hopped into his taxi. Holmes looked out the back window as he opened it and said, "She soon will, and when she does, she will at once know it's important that we speak with her."

"But" Watson began, but Holmes and the taxi were already driving away, the hum of its electric engine rising to a soft whine as it sped away, its engine flaring with blue and white sparks hurtling skywards as it vanished down Baker Street.

SCOTLAND YARD

Inspector Bloodstone looked up from his desk as Watson knocked at the always open door. Inspector Bloodstone may act quite stiff and grumpy much of the time in public and in private, but he was a professional, as well as a good-hearted man. He never shut his door to those who needed his attention or time.

"Come in."

"Oh, it is you, Doctor. Where is Holmes?"

"He thought you might like to be with us."

"Oh, and where might that be?"

"Buckingham Palace."

"Oh!"

Constable Evans entered a moment later.

Inspector Bloodstone swiped a mop of red hair over his eyebrows back over his forehead and nodded to his son, a younger version of himself. Were they the same age, they might be thought twins.

"Get a wagon. We have an appointment with the Queen!" Inspector Bloodstone announced as he rose from behind his desk. He glanced at Watson. "I don't suppose you know why; we are going there?"

Watson shook his head.

Inspector Bloodstone sighed. "Once a Holmes, always a Holmes," he spoke.

Both he and Watson have lived through one more iteration of Holmes, not counting the odd one from the other world who dressed like a cowboy and acted like one... Steampunk Holmes.

BUCKINGHAM PALACE

Holmes and Watson sat at the far end of the Round Table where the knights of King Arthur used to gather in counsel with their King.

Holmes had his pipe resting on the round table, laying on a silver plate, always ready for him.

The Queen frowned on anyone getting her table messy. And pipes were the worst, so she always had a silver tray for him to place his pipe.

Watson sat on the other side of Holmes, with his hat on the table, also on a silver tray.

Inspector Bloodstone and his son, Constable Evans, sat on the opposite side of Holmes, both looking quite solemn at the moment.

And decidedly uncomfortable.

The Good Queen Mary was not one to waste her time on frivolities, so this had to be important, and possibly also dangerous.

Anything that Holmes touched these days seemed to be inextricably tied to a moment of great danger...for someone or their country.

They all seemed distracted, but for varied reasons.

Holmes was curious as to how the Queen would deal with the knowledge; he had earlier given to her in private. He had assumed she would react a certain way, and she had so far. Which is why he had told Watson, in advance, to bring Inspector Bloodstone along as well.

Watson was still somewhat confused about this meeting and definitely upset over losing his date with his dear fiancée, Ms. Hudson.

Holmes pondered his friend a moment. Wondered when the two would just get on with it and announce their wedding date. But so far, both had been mum and quite casual about it.

"A proper rest is important for a man to function…well, like a man," Watson whispered to Holmes.

Holmes chuckled. "And what fair damsel do you refer to, my dear Watson?"

Watson had blushed and shut up. He was quite stubborn when it came to discussing his personal affairs and love life.

And he had shut up, also, because now Good Queen Mary was frowning at him from her side of the table. She was not wearing robes of state, but rather a simple outfit, like one might use for an outing, or an arduous walk through a forest. Her earlier life with Professor Challenger had toughened her up, and also made her less formal than one would expect from an authority figure of her status.

Which Holmes approved of whole heartedly. One should never take oneself too seriously or risk the danger of losing one's soul.

But another man in the room, one General Able Ogre, who sat next the Good Queen Mary, fretted impatiently. Not a likable chap, or a very patient one either. He gave Watson and Holmes deep frowns, and he looked almost as if he were sneering at the Inspector, though his face was constructed in such a way as to give that impression, even when he genuinely smiled.

Neither Holmes nor Watson particularly liked the General. Something neither could put a finger on to be more definite in their distrust and dislike, but no matter what it might turn out to be, the man still chafed on their nerves.

"Can we start now?" General Ogre demanded, a tad irritably, tapping a long, manicured fingernail urgently on the tabletop to emphasis his impatience.

"We best do," Good Queen Mary acknowledged to the General, the hint of distaste in her tone.

He stopped tapping his finger but kept his frown when he looked away from her. He did not notice he was frowning, or else ignored it, since frowning seemed to be a usual characteristic of the man.

Holmes did notice that the man's right eye twitched whenever he looked at the Queen, and even more so, when he looked at him or Watson. He completely ignored Inspector Bloodstone and the Constable Evans. Seeing them as mere public servants and nothing more. Beneath his dignity to pay more than official attention to.

And there he was wrong. The man was so full of himself that he ignored the fact that Holmes could read a man like a book, which Holmes most definitely was at that moment.

Holmes could sense the General's distaste for the Inspector and son and filed that for later thought. This was not the first time he had noticed it, but now was not a time for such personal feelings to be aroused. Especially, at this moment when so much was at stake.

POLITICAL MEETING

Pahalgam, India

Long time ago

Young Sherlock Holmes sat next to his master, the Monk, who wore orange robes this morning, as a sign of his spiritual office, and leaned against a long wooden staff that later Holmes would recognize as the staff of a younger Merlin.

Two older men stood at the front of the large room Sherlock and the Monk sat within. The one on the right was slightly stooped, had hair messed up, and missing teeth. The one on the right stood straight and tall, had a shining face, with bright white teeth and a winning smile.

The man on the right spoke to the audience. "We are here to vote on who shall be the leader of our community this day forward."

The Monk lightly prodded Sherlock's arm. "Watch is eyes. They are windows to the truth."

Holmes nodded and focused on the man's eyes as he spoke.

"Tell me what you see, Sherlock."

Sherlock said in a lowered voice. "I see nothing."

"Exactly."

The man speaking went on. "I promise that I shall bring peace and prosperity to Pahalgam."

"What do you see now, Sherlock?" The Monk asked.

Holmes focused again on the man's eyes. "Nothing."

The second man, older of the two speaking, shuffled a food forward and eyed the community gathered in the large room to listen to his position on becoming leader. "I was born here forty-two years ago after my mother and father were chased from their homes in Delhi by the British Empire. "

The crowd stirred. None particularly liked the British, but they tolerated Sherlock because of his good nature and the kind works he performed for the elderly and the young at times.

One such elderly person sat near Sherlock and gave him a warm smile.

The elderly woman's stomach growled, and she appeared ready to faint.

Sherlock felt the small package of cloth he had carried with him for his lunch and that of the Monk.

He glanced at the Monk, who nodded.

Sherlock quietly slid the package to the elderly woman and partially opened it. Her eyes lit up when she saw the chapatis and rice. Tears began to wet her face.

Sherlock smiled at her and nodded to her.

She lifted the gift and quietly began eating it.

The Monk smiled at Sherlock. Whispered, "We shall eat later; she may not."

Sherlock nodded. "I will run back to the ashram to get more food for her."

He started to get up.

The Monk held him down. "Not yet. I want you to stay for a few more minutes."

"But…"

The Monk shook his head. "It is important what you see now. The viper that is hiding in the brush or the milk cow bursting with fresh milk to share."

The stooped man nodded. "I see you remember our agony. Our loss. Our friends who died. Tortured and murdered like livestock. A nation that stooped to using magic to keep us enslaved."

He leaned closer to the nearest of the crowd and revealed teeth that were decaying in his mouth. "To keep us in darkness. Do not believe everything you hear, even it if is from a kind looking and handsome face. The cobra lays coiled in its basket, waiting for the piper to summon it to attack."

The younger man turned to the older one. "Sir, you mock me."

"I do not. I merely point out the obvious. You are not a bad man...yet. But you burn with the embers of a deep and dark hatred for life. And that shall bring ruin to our Pahalgam if not drowned in time."

The Monk turned to Sherlock again. "Tell me what you see in the older man's eyes, Sherlock."

Sherlock focused on the eyes of the older politician. "I see fire."

"Why do you think that is?"

Holmes frowned in thought.

BUCKINGHAM PALACE

Chamber of the Knights of the Round Table

Now

Good Queen Mary sneezed several times into a silk handkerchief, then set it down in her lap.

Holmes shook his head, his memories fading at the explosion of the queen's sneeze.

No sooner had she done that, than she began to sneeze again.

"Your Majesty, perhaps we should postpone this meeting, since you are not feeling well," suggested General Ogre.

Good Queen Mary was fighting a serious fever and sneezing frequently. All the more reason for all to distance themselves as they were now seated.

Good Queen Mary scowled at the General. "I have battled demons and vampire, werewolves and madmen. I shall not let, not let..."

She began to sneeze again and hurriedly covered her mouth with her handkerchief once more. Then said, "A tiny sneeze get in the way of my work."

Good Queen Mary pushed paperwork in front of her

forward a tad and perused them silently, adjusting her handkerchief to be at the ready as she did so.

Holmes had given the notes to her to read earlier, but she was just now realizing their content's purpose.

"I will never get used to this place," Constable Evans whispered to his father, Inspector Bloodstone.

Good Queen Mary looked up from her notes and gave Constable Evans a sweet smile. "My dear, sweet, Constable Evans, which makes two of us. This place reeks of magic and sweat!"

She grinned. "Manly sweat!"

Constable Evans blushed at her attention. She gave him a new warm smile.

Holmes grinned. "I rather think that Harry would be quite fond of being here. Manly smell or no."

Good Queen Mary grinned back at him. "Oh, he is. Sometimes I let him wander down here just for the fun of it."

"Harry claims it powers him up. Whatever in bloody hell that means!" She snorted with a deep throated laugh that reminded everyone there, except the General Ogre, of Professor Challenger's huge, throaty laughs.

Laughs which were both loud, as well as quite

infectious. Only good-hearted people can laugh and make a person feel warm inside and happy to be with them like that. And Good Queen Mary and Professor Challenger were two such good souls.

Then Good Queen Mary began sneezing again.

The General backed away somewhat. He took the brunt of the sneezes, not being allowed to sit anywhere, but next to the Good Queen Mary.

It was that moment that Holmes realized why the General had sparked such a degree of mistrust and dislike for him. His eyes! There was fire in them.

POLITICAL MEETING

Pahalgam, India

Long time ago

The older man smiled triumphantly as the crowd of people raised him on their shoulders. He no longer looked as stooped, nor as old as he was carried from the building to be given a victor parade.

He had won the post of leader.

The Monk turned to Sherlock as they both rose. "Hurry back to the ashram for the food, and I will make sure our friend makes it safely home."

Sherlock nodded and left by the back entrance to the building. He circled the building to the left and ran a block to find the suspension bridge that crossed the roaring Ganges.

He ran across it, heading for the long path to the ashram and the kitchen where even now the young students like him were preparing for dinner.

BOULDER

Next Ganges River

Pahalgam, Night

Sherlock gazed at the village of Pahalgam where flames tortured the night and screams could be heard above the roar of the Ganges.

"It is done."

Sherlock did not react. He just stared at the horror of what was happening.

The Monk sat next to him and put a warm hand on Sherlock's shoulder. "Do not take it personally, Sherlock. Man has freewill. He can choose his own fate. And our friends below have chosen theirs."

Sherlock asked the question burning so brightly in his heart now. He turned to look into the Monk's face. "Why? Why would they fight one another like this? They are neighbors and friends, family, brothers, and sister."

The Monk shut his eyes a moment, then opened them.

"Remember when I asked you to tell me what you saw in the eyes of the two political men?"

"I do."

"Tell me why I asked that?"

Sherlock frowned. The Monk always turned his answers into questions for Sherlock to figure out.

He shut his eyes and allowed the anguish of his vision to dim, the cries of pain and suffering to diminish, and then floated in a soft, gentle awareness. He felt time flee by. The Monk did nothing to disturb him.

Sherlock opened his eyes after long time. His breathing, which had been accelerating at the sight of the fight in the village, was now slowed. His dry throat was moist again and the tears that had wet his eyes were now dry.

"Master."

"Yes, Sherlock."

"The older man burned with the desire for power and control."

"And?"

"And the younger man was his stooge."

Sherlock jumped up. He felt anger returning again. "It was all fake. They were never opposing each other. Never!"

The Monk rose. "Persons speak often of the snake waiting to pounce when you least expect it to, but it not the snakes we need fear the most."

Sherlock nodded. "It is greed and selfish ambition."

The Monk smiled.

They turned to leave the comfortable boulder they often used to mull problems over, or just to relax and listen to the rush of the Ganges.

"Master."

"Yes, Sherlock?"

"I will not be like them."

The Monk smiled.

BUCKINGHAM PALACE

Chamber of the Knights of the Round Table

Now

Holmes smiled, but not obviously at the General's discomfort. Sometimes, he thought that Good Queen Mary was deliberately torturing the man, though why, he could not figure out.

Yet.

"I suppose I should be forthright about why I've summoned all of you here of you here."

"That would be nice, your majesty," General Ogre agreed.

Holmes and Watson said nothing, being more generous

with the Queen and her needs and respectful. Another reason both found General Ogre lacking character as well as some other element they had yet to isolate.

Good Queen Mary arched an eyebrow in irritation at General Ogre's impudence. "Archbishop O'Reilly was found dead in his room last night."

Holmes tensed. "By what means?"

"Spector!"

Holmes let his breath out in a quick burst of exasperation. "Drat that dark soul. Has he nothing better to do than harm the innocent?"

General Ogre shrugged. "What does it matter, Detective Holmes? Innocent or not, he has struck again."

"Again?" Holmes asked, having paid close attention to the way General Ogre emphasized again.

"Yes, the Queen did not tell you, knowing I would. This is but one of many such deaths about the city these last several nights. The newspapers have been told to post nothing until we have resolved this issue."

Watson played with his hat, plainly distressed by the news. "We should have been told sooner."

"The General felt that you two had enough on your hands already."

Watson glared at the General. "Oh, did he now?"

"The usual marks?" Holmes inquired, not losing momentum on what was crossing his mind that moment. And also cutting Watson short before his temper got the best of him. He had read every newspaper this morning and knew of the repeated worrisome deaths.

Not by what had been printed about them, but what had not been printed. Instead of deaths, the persons were reported as missing and a request for any information regarding the individuals was attached to the disclosures.

That is when he knew that the Good Queen Mary had a hand in it all.

Good Queen Mary nodded. "Yes, the mark of a knife thrust through his heart, but no blade found."

Holmes scrunched his eyebrows together. "You have a ride waiting for us?"

Good Queen Mary nodded to Constable Evans, who rose. "I will be your ride, Holmes."

"What about me?" General Ogre asked with a frown. "Why am I here if they are going and I am not?"

Good Queen Mary gave the General an annoyed look. "Your Queen should not have to explain her every motive."

The chamber grew even colder than it already was.

SCOTLAND YARD

Holmes and Watson were escorted into the small office of Inspector Bloodstone. The man is studying the photo of a dead woman as they enter.

He ignores them, continues to study the photo, and make notes with a Bic pen in red ink. On the photo.

He does not notice that both Constable Evans who hao has brought Holmes, John, and Watson inside are standing, waiting for him to acknowledge them.

Constable Evans and Watson wince every time the Inspector makes a new red ink note on the photo. Only Holmes seems unperturbed by the unseemly marks.

Constable Evans clears his throat.

"Yes?" Inspector Bloodstone speaks up, not looking at them or stopping making notes on the photo.

He almost seems like a man possessed at the moment by some invisible force guiding His hand.

"Inspector," Constable Evans speaks once more.

Inspector Bloodstone eyed the photograph in front of him and nodded. "Please, gentlemen, have a seat. As you can see, I am quite the busy man at the moment."

Inspector Bloodstone finishes, nods in satisfaction, then looks up and gives them all a blunt smile. "But I can spare a moment."

Watson laughs.

"What's so funny, Doctor?"

"You asked us to come!"

"Oh, I did, did I?"

Inspector Bloodstone eyes Constable Evans a moment, then shrugs. "I suppose it's my better half intervening on my less so."

Holmes smiled. "Constable Evans is a good officer, Inspector. I fully expect him to become one of your finest detectives in the near future."

Constable Evans blushes.

Watson snickers.

Constable Evans eyes him sternly, but Watson continues to snicker.

"Well then," Inspector Bloodstone speaks up. "I suppose it's to business then."

He shoves the photo towards Holmes.

"You've been watching me like a hawk, so what do you think?"

THE COLD ROOM

Holmes and Watson hover over Henrietta's body, both examining the wound in her chest, cloth hiding the rest of her body from view.

Watson snips a sample of her hair, then a fingernail, then takes scrapings of her skin.

Holmes's attention is solely on the ragged incision on Henrietta's right breast. He uses a cotton probe to poke at the wound, and it descends deep.

He gently pulls it out, a frown appearing on his face as he looks at the tip of the probe.

"Watson, see this."

Watson hands over his samples to a lab tech, who nods and heads for the lab to examine the samples with the advanced equipment they carry there.

"What?"

Holmes hands Watson a fresh cotton probe. "I want you to probe the wound."

Watson takes the probe and gently inserts it into the woman's breast, then frowns. "There are no broken bones from what I can tell. But I am sure the x-rays will tell a different story."

"Perhaps," Holmes replies.

Holmes rubs the rough beard on his jaw. He did not shave this morning. Which is quite unusual for him. A cause of alarm to Watson, but one he would keep to himself. Holmes rarely did such things without good reason.

Holmes smiles. "Who would ever have thought such exemplary tools would be ordinary forensic tools one day."

"You mean the present, don't you? I have to admit, that even though Jules and Wells are not medical doctors, they have quite the grasp of our needs."

Holmes smiles. "Those two never seem to run out of ideas that surprise me."

"Well, considering they have fought Martians off our world, and traveled back and forth in time to reconstruct our future, which doesn't surprise me, so much."

Holmes nodded. "True, but sometimes I wonder if there isn't another Earth...one unlike this one, where they didn't save the world...where..."

His voice caught.

Watson patted Holmes's arm. "I seriously doubt that God would let any world be created where we two didn't exist...together."

Holmes chuckled. "I suppose that is so. But this present

sometimes feels like our future at one time."

Watson briefly felt a tug on his heart.

Holmes senses his friend's sudden distress. "I am sorry. We need to stick to business. All this fancy talk about time travel and parallel worlds can confuse and distress anyone after a time."

Watson shakes his head. "The past is like a shadow that follows us everywhere. Everywhere we go there are shadows of the past. A street no longer with gas lamps, but electric. A pub we used to frequent now a supermarket with electronic cash registers."

Holmes nods. "One thing I will never complain about is this new-fangled phone that Edison and Tesla produced. I rather fancy being able to call anywhere now with this tiny device."

He took out his cell phone. It had a two-inch screen, flaps that closed with curtains embroidered on them. Good Queen Mary's face was inscribed on the back metal.

"I am sure the Queen gets more of a kick out of these than we, Holmes. Did you know that you can access the entire wealth of human knowledge on this small device?"

Holmes placed a thumb against the screen of his cell phone. I do not think I would like to try reading it on this device,

though."

Watson barked with laughter "That's big enough to club an elephant over the head with, Holmes."

Watson sighs. He turns to Holmes. "All those years ago and yet it seems just like yesterday, doesn't it? Which reminds me, we should see if James Moriarty has one. Be nice to chat with him again."

"Suspect he's still in Fairie with the love of his life."

Watson wipes at a tear in his right eye. "Drat it all, Holmes, look what you have done now. I can spoil the evidence if my tears strike her breast."

Watson steps back.

Pulling the probe out as he does.

He gives it a surprised look. "No blood!"

"No blood."

"But that's impossible, Holmes." Watson double checks Holmes's face. "But you knew that, did you not?"

"So is the manner of the wound. No earthly weapon I am familiar with can make such a ragged wound and yet exit without a single drop of blood."

"It's as if her blood were frozen."

Holmes and Watson eye each other, the same thought crossing their minds the exact same time."

ARCHBISHOP O'REILLY

Sherlock Holmes and Watson are let into the Abbey through a side door. They pass two Priests standing guard at the door's entrance.

General Ogre guides them through a winding series of corridors, dank with moisture, and in some spots showing signs of moss making gains on the walls between the ancient stones forming then.

Then they reached the underground level, after several descending flights of roughly hewn stone steps to arrive at a new corridor that sopped shortly where a rough-faced man with a stern look to him eyed Holmes and Watson in an unfriendly manner.

General Ogre smiled. "Don't let Mason disturb either of you, he is my personal guard."

"But why do you have a guard over a dead man?" Watson asked.

"Because this is not just an ordinary dead body in there. Come, you will see. Let us in, Mason."

Mason muttered something below the audible range but opened the massive door shutting them out.

The crypt was one of the older ones, reserved for the

royalty of the Church. Only Bishops and Archbishops were interred here, even if temporarily.

"Thank you, Mason. Let us you and I take a short walk to give these gentlemen some time to examine His Grace."

Mason nodded and he and General Ogre exited, the massive door shutting behind them, its huge mass scraping the floor with a low vibration that sent Watson's teeth to be grinding.

"I hate these places. Nothing built well. You would think with all the wealth they steal from the common man they would at least build good doors."

Holmes chuckled. "If they were too good, it would be too hard to know when someone was where they should not be."

Watson turned to Holmes. The ring of candles about the archbishop's sheeted body cast dancing shadows on Holmes's face. "Why would anyone even want to come down this far, let along try to steal anything?"

Holmes smiled. "Curiosity killed the cat. Ever been that way. It is what has driven man since the caveman days. Though I rather suspect there never were cavemen as they are often portrayed in history books."

"Or scientific journals," Watson added.

"Agreed. Science rarely acknowledges the truths that make one uncomfortable. And our world has many undesirable truths that make lies of history."

Watson nodded.

He went to the corpse and gently pulled back the cloth until it revealed his wound. "I've seen this kind of wound before, Holmes."

"As have I."

"Lady Henrietta."

"Indeed. And our thoughts about India have now run full circle."

"Yes. I saw the same when I was in China as well," Watson declared. "In the Himalayas."

"It's a rare dagger used by only certain tribal warriors of the High Steppes."

"Ice dagger to be precise," Holmes concluded.

Watson reached into his black medical bag, which he kept with him at all times. He took out a pair of rubber gloves, then a short probe of metal. He began pushing and pulling, opening, and pushing into the wound as he began from the lower part of the archbishop's chest until it ended just below his neck."

"Nasty wound."

"Indeed. Much more so than Lady Henrietta."

"Which would make me think that a personal debt was being paid back in this case."

"His assistant was driven mad by the poor man's screams and when he saw the body, he went utterly insane," Holmes added.

Watson shook his head. "He must have been quite close to the archbishop."

Holmes nodded. "And your conclusion now, Watson?"

"The same. Ice dagger."

"May I?" Holmes requested.

Watson nodded and stepped aside.

Holmes took a vial out of Watson's medical bag and a pipette, which he used to catch some pieces of flesh that were still moist within the wound.

He put the pipette into the vial and stoppered it. "Once we return to Baker Street, I will perform a final and conclusive analysis."

"And then?"

Holmes pulled the sheet back over the archbishop's pale white body, then handed Watson his black medical bag.

"Ask me again once I am through."

SHADOWS WITHIN SHADOWS

His face might have been used for a sculpture it was so pure looking and unblemished, but once he turns to look at you, as he did at Squire Jones, the beauty faded like a candle snuffed from existence. This man's eyes burned, but not with the brightness of intelligence, or of beauty, but instead of deep, dark foul realms that soil the soul.

Squire Evans looked quickly away. No man who dared to stare into this man's face for any length of time remained in this world for long.

The Maestro, as he called himself, hated his looks as much as Narcissus loved his own. Why? No one knew. He would never discuss this hatred. But it exuded from him like a foul stench. And the thick muscled fellow covered every inch of his body two to three times over with clothing to hide every inch of his skin possible.

The oddest part of this habit was he never sweat. Not once. Not even when he led his men into action. Even when his men were sweating profusely from sweltering heat, the Maestro never showed one drop of sweat through his clothing.

And of his face, only his eyes were visible because of a thick mask he wore with thin eye slits. He needed to see, but sometimes, especially in bright light, he would draw a dark threaded mask over his eyes so that not even his eyes were visible. He could still see through it, but no one could see if he were looking at them.

A terror device, for sure. The Maestro was exceptionally skilled in instill terror into the strongest of hearts. But Squire Jones new the extra layer was also another layer of self-protection.

Maestro turned to Squire Jones. "And you're sure that Detective Holmes is now on the case?"

"I am. I overheard one of the constables talking about it with another at their favorite pub, which you have me frequent."

Maestro nodded. "Good. Perhaps, I have done well in giving you so much freedom."

Squire Jones half bowed his head. "It is my honor, Maestro."

"Indeed, it is."

Maestro turned to another man who had been standing silently at the rear of the dark room he and Squire Jones stood within. "You will follow the plans I have outlined precisely. Am I understood?"

The man raised a fist with his left arm over his heart and half bowed his head. "Maestro!" He exclaimed and rushed from the dark room.

"This time your plan will work, Maestro."

Maestro turned to Squire Jones. He gestured to a large stone box. "If what I have inside this box does not stop him, then I don't know what will."

"Worried, Maestro?"

Maestro glares at Squire Jones, his eyes burning with hatred. "I burn with it. And when I burn with it, someone must pay the price."

Maestro went for the way out. "Pray it is not you that pays that price!"

He vanished into the dark outside.

Squire Jones eyed the stone box and shuddered. "I do, Maestro, I do."

Then he followed Maestro from the room.

MONK

Pahalgam

Early Morning

High up in the Himalayas

Young Holmes sits on the edge of a steep drop alongside the Monk, a holy man rumored to be over a hundred years old, but strong as an ox.

Both have their eyes closed.

"Om!" Hums the monk.

Holmes listens to the sound but does not utter it.

The monk stops. Opens his eyes.

Holmes does not open his.

"I want you to wait until you can no longer hear me, then open your eyes."

"Then what?" Holmes asks.

"Use your imagination."

"What if I have none?"

The monk laughs. Gets up and begins walking away. The monk reaches about ten feet away, then takes a turn behind a huge boulder. He reaches into a pouch at his hip, strapped by worn leather and reaches into it.

He pulls a small Cobra from the pouch and closes it.

Caresses the cobra gently, kisses it lightly on its head, then sets it on the ground.

It begins wiggling away, towards Holmes.

221B BAKER STREET

Watson sat on the front porch, ruminating on thoughts he told Holmes he would rather forget. But no matter how hard he relegated them to a lost past, to moments he can never relive, still he treasures them.

Images of the woman who saved him from freezing to death. It has been over a year now since he found Holmes and almost half a year more since he returned to a London, he had almost forgotten.

And in the last half year many memories were coming back to him.

His good friend, Professor Langford, also known as the Invisible Man, had said that might happen. And it was. He frowned at the thought of that scoundrel who sold out his good friend, Holmes to Moriarty. Allowing poor Holmes to be tortured without even knowing he was being done so.

Moriarty! He almost banged his fist on the hard stone of the porch, but caught himself when he heard the door behind him open.

"Watson, breaking your hand on the past is never a good idea."

Watson thrust the offending hand into his coat pocket and scooted over for Holmes to sit next him. Which Holmes did. They both sat in silence a long time, then Holmes commented. "I understand that where the old pub used to be is now a great French café."

"I don't like French food," Watson declared.

"The chef specializes in a certain cuisine I thought you might find especially likable."

"Doubt it"

"Truly, I would not lie to you, John."

Watson gives Holmes an apologetic glance. "Sorry. You could very well be right. But right now, the only thing attractive to me is finding the chaps behind the murders we are investigating. It is dreadful. Simply dreadful that modern man has learned nothing from the past."

Holmes chuckled. "Oh! They have learned all right. How to copy the past and improve upon its cruelty."

Watson sighed. "Sadly so." He glanced at Holmes, who unlike him, was smiling. "Why are you so dratted cheerful for, Holmes. Just because you proved our theory that it was an ice dagger, does nothing to help us find the perpetrator. Or to soothe my ravaging stomach!"

Watson's stomach chose that moment to growl loudly.

Holmes patted Watson on his left knee, rose. "Come, let us go eat."

"One question before we leave."

"Yes?"

"Why do you believe that Spector is behind all of this. After all, ice daggers are not that obscure in the history of the criminal world."

"True. But London is not part of that history, or that world."

Watson rose. "Where to?"

"Chevz Lefaivre."

"I told you I hate French food."

"Oh, but you shall like this food."

"Why would I"

"Croissants and sweet tarts are their specialty."

Watson's eyes widened with excitement. "Holmes, I could kiss you." Then quickly. "I mean my stomach, which is."

"Save the kisses until after I have treated you to their scones. I hear they rival Ms. Hudson's."

"That'll be the day," Watson declared as he followed Holmes down the steps to the sidewalk. "Never happen."

A FATAL BLOW

General Ogre exits Buckingham Palace and heads to his electric car, where his driver awaits him.

The driver is leaning against the front hood, apparently smoking.

"You know I find smoking distasteful!" He admonishes the driver.

The driver turns around.

But it is not who the General expects to see.

It is as if the man he saw unfolds from himself and expands outwards and upwards, black strings and white stripes of light exuding from his body.

"I am come for you, General Ogre."

The General's scream startles the guards at the front gate and the doors of Buckingham palace.

When they rush to the General's car, they find him slumped to the ground, on his back, eyes staring into infinity. A tear is over his chest. Where his heart is.

But there is no blood.

CHEVZ LEFAIVRE

Watson clutches a soft cloth bag filled with scones, tarts, and croissants. He rubs his stomach with his free hand as he stops at the edge of the sidewalk to wait for Holmes.

Holmes joins him. "Well?" Holmes asks.

"Well, what"

Holmes smiles. Watson is too stubborn to admit he was wrong. And Holmes has no need to prove he is right, because Watson is carrying the proof of Holmes's logic already...in the lovely, gift bag in Watson's right hand and in a stomach that no longer growls with hunger.

Holmes felt a familiar warmth touch his heart. While, he has spent many years letting Watson guess about his feelings, which he had more than enough of, he felt a reluctance now to hide them.

Was the past finally changing him? Or just catching up.

Especially, in light of what they had both gone through...for each other, and those they loved.

"Did you like them?"

Watson shook his head. "Drat it all, Holmes. I bought a dozen, did I not?"

And that was the end of that.

221B BAKER STREET

Holmes and Watson climb from an electric taxi, and it drives off, bright sparks of light flaring from its roof turbine. They head for the front porch but are surprised to see three old friends standing there, waiting for them.

"Greetings!" Professor Challenger calls to them. "About time you two stopped playing around."

"Are those scones in your bag, Watson?" Conan asks.

"I doubt even my magic could pry one lose from our friend, Watson, Conan," Harry remarks with a grin. "Judging by the way he is gripping that bag; I suspect it would mean war to even try.

Watson clutches his bag tighter. "Really!"

Harry nods. "The truth will out, dear friend."

Holmes laughs. "True enough, Harry, but not the scones in Watson's bag. They have a mind to stay put right where they are."

Everyone breaks into laughter.

Watson blushes.

Harry Houdini, tall, with his brown skin and hair. Professor Challenger with his fiery red beard and red lion's mane hair capping a huge, muscular body and Conan seated on the top step, smiling break into further laughter.

Watson grunts, clutches his bag tighter to his chest. "Not sharing. That is my final word! What do you scoundrels want this time of night?"

Holmes glanced beyond them, then back to the street where he spotted a familiar police wagon.

Constable Evans exited the building, eating a fresh scone. "Well about time you two showed up."

"What's going on?" Watson asked once more. "Can't a man get a moment's peace?"

Holmes answered for Constable Evans. "I believe our good Constable Evans is here to deliver us to the Yard and our friends are tagging along."

Watson sighed. "Obviously, not for the fun of it.

Harry is first down from the porch and claps a hand on Watson's shoulder. "Fun is just a point of view."

"You would say that!"

Everyone laughed at that as they all headed for Constable Evans's police wagon.

COLD ROOM

Scotland Yard

Later

Harry, Professor Challenger, and Conan stand at the exit of the room, watching silently as Watson finishes his autopsy.

Inspector Bloodstone and his son, Constable Evans, stand at the other end of the room, also watching. Inspector Bloodstone's eyes are bloodshot as if he has been drinking, but it is just fatigue catching up.

"Well?" Inspector Bloodstone demands.

"Just a moment," Doctor Watson demands back in an irritable voice. He caught Harry and Conan dipping into his cloth bag of scones and croissants while he was working and was even more angry now that he had less to return home to.

Harry finished the last scone. "These scones are marvelous, Holmes, wherever in the world did you find something so good in London?"

"Shut up! I'm trying to concentrate," Watson blared at him. *Now the blaggarts will probably empty the café before I can purchase more!*

Harry gave Holmes a wink and a smile to Professor Challenger but said no more.

Finally, Watson finished his autopsy. "Ice Dragger."

Inspector Bloodstone frowned. "What in God's name is a bloody ice dagger?"

Watson ignores the Inspector and gestures to his friend and partner, Holmes. "Holmes?" Watson turned to him. "Your observation?"

"Same cut over the right side of the heart, and a twist and plunge into the right ventricle of the heart."

"But why don't the blasted bodies bleed?" Inspector Bloodstone roars. "It is obvious no vampire did this. There would be fang marks on General Ogre's throat, were that so."

He turned to Holmes. "So why not?"

Holmes nodded to Harry. "I think someone here is more qualified to answer that than I might endeavor to clarify for you, Inspector."

"Humphh!"

"As you know, Inspector the luckless souls who have been murdered in this strange manner...all showed no loss of blood at the crime scene. All, now even this one, have the same brutal, cunning cut to their hearts."

Harry nodded. "As Holmes is trying to say, magic!"

"Why magic?

"Inspector," Harry speaks. "For the ice to from a dagger and yet remain strong enough to pierce the ribcage and enter the heart, it would have to be as hard as stone, but to leave no trace of itself afterwards."

"It would have to be able to dissolve…like ice," the Inspector added. Eyes lighting up. "God on Earth. What fiendishness."

"Dark magic always is, Inspector, sorry to say," Harry says. "Which is why Holmes asked for my help in this."

"And mine, because of the history of such weapons," Challenger speaks up."

"And mine," Conan adds, "Because I have spent many years off and on in the frozen south, where such weapons were created at one time."

Inspector Bloodstone turns to Conan. "I did not know that."

"That is because my wife and I are not very prone to discuss our private lives, as the rest of these chaps."

Holmes chuckles. "Assuming one has such."

Watson snorts with laughter.

Harry laughs. "I love everything I do to be seen by the public."

"You would!" Watson accuses, but with a smile. "I imagine Merlin must roll over in his grave knowing what a show-off you are."

"He has no grave and even if he did, he would not roll over, as he is the one who taught me to always be honest about what you love." Harry grins broadly. "And I love attention."

"And helping people," Conan speaks up."

"Thank you, Conan."

You're welcome."

"Will you clowns please stop with the jokes and just tell me what is going on? I have a job to do here and no time for such fiddle faddle as you are doing."

Constable Evans stifles a laugh. "Harry, please before father has a heart attack of impatience."

The Inspector glares at his son, then shakes his head. "Surrounded by idiots."

"And fortunately for you, Inspector, knowledgeable ones"

Harry steps to the front of the room, next to the body and holds his right palm over the incision made by the ice dagger. His palm begins to glow a bright red. "Most definitely magic. And the worst kind."

"I thought all dark magic was the worst kind," Inspector Bloodstone snorted.

"No, there are levels, even in the darkest of magic."

Harry removed his hand to look at Professor Challenger. "When you called upon us for help, Holmes, I made a point of it for the three of us to visit the Royal Museum to examine some artifacts found in the Antiquities section."

"And with my superior knowledge of ancient archaeology," Challenger explained, "it was just a matter of a few minutes before we discovered what we needed to learn."

"And?" Inspector Bloodstone demanded, almost growling in frustration. Knowing a lecture was on its way, it irritated him even more than having to deal with one more dark wizard prowling the streets of London and killing off prominent citizens.

ROYAL MUSEUM OF LONDON

Antiquities Section

Earlier

Challenger, Conan, and Harry stand facing a large door, which has arcane symbols carved about its rim. The symbols are dull looking to the mortal eye, but to Harry's eye, he can see the magical wards spun about each of them to secure the entrance.

Even Harry would have a challenging time entering without permission through this door.

"Knock again, Conan."

Conan eyes Challenger. "You're bigger stronger than I am, you do it!"

Challenger laughs. "But the words above the door say only the meek may open the door"

Conan fumes angrily. "I am not weak!"

"I said, meek, not weak,' Challenger corrected his friend.

Conan sighed. "Very well, but if I am turned into a toad, I will be quite unhappy about it."

Harry grins. "Don't worry, Conan, this is not that kind of magical door."

Harry moves past Conan and knocks lightly on the door.

Nothing happens.

He knocks again.

Nothing.

Finally, he turns to Conan. "It appears I am not meek or weak."

Challenger chuckles merrily. "Conan, please, you're the only one here who can..."

Conan rushes forward and pounds on the door.

COOL ROOM

Scotland Yard

Later

"I see," Inspector Bloodstone speaks.

He turns to Harry. "But even so, how does this arcane…uh, ice dagger. How does it manage to kill a person by itself?"

"It does not."

"My men claim they saw an intense glow about the General as he was screaming."

Harry spoke up, a sadness in his voice. "Unfortunately, there is more to an ice dagger, than mere history and legend."

"How so?"

"Inspector, only one device I know of can do this evil work."

"Yes yes, on with it!" Inspector Bloodstone demands.

"It requires a familiar."

"Then there was a Spector involved," Inspector Bloodstone exclaims.

"Which explains why the victim, in this case a decorated war hero and hardly incapable of dealing with a violent situation, was so easily overcome. The terror froze his logic and limbs from functioning properly," Conan stated.

Challenger eyed his friend. "Conan, you do still have a doctor in there, after all."

Conan scowled. "Which I might be doing right now if not for you dragging me along on another supernatural hunt!"

Conan gave Holmes a roll of his eyes. "Nothing personal, Holmes."

Of course not, Conan. I most certainly respect you as a friend, a doctor and a man determined to help the innocent."

Challenger gave Conan a warm smile. "And without you, dear Conan, my life would be a vacuum."

"Indeed," Holmes adds gently.

Challenger sighs, then pats Harry on his shoulder. "Harry here tells me that whoever has the device can summon a Spector that resembles the worst nightmare of whoever is targeted."

"And" Harry cuts in. "Makes ii possible for the terrified person to be stabbed by the ice dagger without being seen, as the Spector demands all the attention of anyone watching."

"Damned hideously clever," Inspector Bloodstone sighs. "Sickens my soul."

Constable Evans puts a hand on his father's arm to comfort him. "Thanks son," Inspector Bloodstone tells Constable Evans. "I wish you didn't have to live in such a horrid world as this."

"It's not horrid as long as people like you and our friends here exist."

Inspector Bloodstone did an exceedingly rare thing for him. He showed public affection by hugging Constable Evans for a long time, eyes tearing up. "Truly, you are a gift of the gods to this tired old man."

Everyone is silent.

Finally, the Inspector lets go, then turns to the men in the room. "So, Harry, continue with your visit to the Museum."

ROYAL MUSEUM OF LONDON

Department of Antiquities

Earlier

Head Curator, Henry Styles looked at the three men who stood outside his now open door and frowned. "You realize this is utterly impossible to explain to anyone?"

Harry Houdini waved his right hand in dismissal of the thought, a blue glow emanating momentarily from his palm as it flew past Henry's face.

"I'm sure that Good Queen Mary of Scots, whom, by the way, sent us, would find it quite the opposite and no inconvenience whatsoever."

Henry paled, not at the use of the blue magic, but at the mention of the Queen's name. He crossed himself and made a respectful sign towards the direction of Buckingham Palace. "Well then, shall we to it?" He asked, as if he had planned nothing different from the beginning.

No one believed his act, but he did, and that is all that mattered. They were going to get inside the one place that no one but the Queen's most trusted emissaries ever traveled.

Deeper even than the Seven Doors to Hell, as the entrance to another hidden chamber was called.

Not waiting for an answer and also to hide the deeper flush of color returning to his face and the nervous twitches of his eyebrows which always happened when he was scared, Henry opened the door wider to admit Professor Challenger, Harry and Conan into the most secret and deeply hidden part of the Antiquities section of the Royal Museum.

"Please do hurry, the constables are due to patrol past any moment now this side of the building and I don't want them poking their nose into my business as well!"

He glared at them, "And they most definitely would not have the Queen's permission to enter where you gentlemen are going!"

And as if those last words of warning gave a final relief to his soul, Henry returned to the direction he was headed, urging them on with a motion of his right hand, to follow.

Harry and his friends entered, all doing their best not to show the hint of a smile at what they knew was really going on.

As Harry passed the Curator, his left hand flew out with a fistful of tickets to his new show at the Globe Theater,

which had sold out weeks ago.

The Curator, without looking down, snatched them hurriedly and stuffed them into his right pants pocket, shut the door, then guided them for a second door, already open, with a long corridor in view and many torch conches lit and burning brightly.

Conan eyed the route before them. "Challenger, does this not remind you of a certain adventure we had some time back."

Challenger growled. "The Seven Doors to Hell is certainly a very apt moniker for where we ended up that time."

Conan shivered. "I would never have thought Good Queen Mary of Scots so devious to construct such a route, and then arm it with so much horror and terrors."

Challenger laughed. "Ah, Conan, when she was younger, and she and I danced the sands of distant China and swam the channels of the India Isles, she was much more terrifying then."

"How so?"

Challenger lowered his voice. "If I told you, she would kill you."

"Why me and not you?"

"And that's why I can't tell you!"

Henry turned about. "Would you two stop chattering like a pair of chipmunks. This is serious business we are upon."

Harry chuckled. "Just be glad they are not married. It would be far worse!"

"Hey!" Challenger roared.

Conan snickered but said nothing further.

"This way. This way!" Henry urged everyone.

They followed in silence as the Curator wound them through one long dank, musty smelling corridor after the other, past rusting suits of armor, hanging spears and swords, mandalas made of gold and iron, jeweled pendants hanging on gloved hands of armor, battle axes of marble and of wood, helmets with skeleton heads peering out, hanging from chains.

The utter terror of the corridors, let alone their dank, musty, and often quite dark nature, were both terrifying and utterly dispelling of any desire for further humor form the men. It felt as if they were leaving a sane world into a much darker and even, insane one...where hobgoblins, demons, sprites, twinkles, and trolls oozed, pawed, haunted, and flew on skeleton horses, fairy dust wings and paws of iron sharp blades.

Down steps deeply rutted from centuries of use and swollen from the sweat of moisture from the waters of the Thames leaking underground into the structure. Then right to a new corridor, which switched back and forth, like a horse trying to throw its rider, and even further they went along where the air smelled of brine and ancient rot, then along a narrower corridor, ceiling so low that poor Challenger was constantly scraping his scalp on it.

It all finally ended in a brightly lit room.

Challenger rubbed his bruised head; Harry brushed his suit off...the dust in places had been so thick he had to blow his nose to clear its passages.

Conan, hungry, pulled an apple Jean had given him earlier to eat.

Challenger elbowed Conan lightly in the side. "Hoped we'd never see this dratted place again."

Conan sighed deeply "If we had a sovereign for every hope that was banished utterly, we would be richer than the Queen!"

Harry smiled. "No one is richer in England than the Queen."

The Curator lightened up at the jest. "Surely, that is a great understatement, as truly no one in the world could possibly be richer, as she owns our continent from one end to the other."

He whispered confidentially. "She is not only a great administrator of our country, but a quite clever businesswoman as well!"

"I'll second that," Challenger agreed. "I never gamble with her. I always lose."

Henry nodded, then waved at the vast wealth of the room spread before them. "Kindly do not touch anything as we cross through this room. The auditors have special wards about the coin and jewelry which will follow you until your death."

Conan glanced hurriedly at Harry, who lightly shook his head. Conan gave Harry a nod and grin in return.

"Ah! Here we are." The Curator stopped at a plain door, knocked on it. The door opened. A flood of golden light flushed out, drowning the men in its embrace.

"And if this gentleman cannot answer your questions and solve your anxious minds queries, I doubt any can."

A tall man with a youthful face, long white hair and beard stopped stroking the head of his white owl, set it upon his right shoulder, rose from his simple wooden chair, then took a long wooden staff that was still carved arcane runes, and topped by a living leaf.

"Harry!" He greeted. "Long time no see."

Harry did not wait. He dropped to the floor and kneeled before the great magician standing before him. His mentor and master, Merlin the Sager, the White, the Master of Magic.

SCOTLAND YARD

Inspector Bloodstone's Office

Later

"And of course, he was most gracious. He offered us fresh mint and magic herbal tea, then a quick tour of his home in Camelot. We even met four of the junior magicians there. Young Enforcers in the making," Challenger added.

Conan nodded. "Right smart young sorts they are. Quite impressed."

"Got a kick out of the talking toadstool,' Harry admitted. "Quite charming fellow." Harry frowned a moment in thought. "Though, he was quite embarrassing when he had to emit gas."

"Emit gas?" Inspector Bloodstone asked.

Constable Evans made a farting sound.

Everyone looked at him then broke into laughter.

Inspector Bloodstone shook his head. "Son, you never fail to amaze me. Or amuse at times."

"Well, you are much louder than..."

Inspector Bloodstone cleared his throat loudly.

Constable Evans shut up at once.

Holmes smiled. The two were an amazing pair.

Harry folded his hands into his lap and lapsed into silence.

Inspector Bloodstone had to admit it, Harry was a magician unlike any other. Any man who could name the great Merlin as his friend and visit a man who rarely surfaced to greet the world, was indeed, both lucky and blessed.

The Inspector, entranced despite his ill temper, eyed Harry. "Well, finish your dratted story."

"Cannot."

"And just why is that?"

"Because if I told you what happened next, Good Queen Mary would be paying you a prompt visit."

Inspector Bloodstone paled.

Challenger leaned forward, "And trust me, when I say, Inspector, that there are more than seven doors to hell in that dratted museum and we passed them all. Did we not, dear Conan?

Conan, who had fallen asleep during the narration, put a hand over his mouth as he yawned. "Whatever you say, Challenger. Whatever you say."

"The long and the short of it then," Holmes spoke, "Is that my good friends here found what we need to solve this crime of murder and occult terror."

"And what is that?" Inspector Bloodstone demanded.

Holmes lifted a small metal box with wires twisted about its base and protruding from its top. "This."

The Inspector reached to take it.

The box opened and the room lit with an ominous presence.

A Spector rose from the tabletop above the box and eyed Inspector Bloodstone with terribly red bloodshot eyes. "I have come for you, Inspector Bloodstone!"

Inspector Bloodstone shot out of his chair. Face pale as a ghost, teeth chattering in terror.

Holmes quickly folded his hands about the box and the vision of the Spector vanished.

"Satisfied, Inspector? Holmes asked.

Inspector Bloodstone was speechless.

No one laughed at his reaction.

Each person in the room had seen an image that they feared the most in their lives and in their nightmares.

But Holmes had just resolved a test given to him by the Monk some time back.

MONK

Pahalgam

Early Morning

High up in the Himalayas

Holmes, without opening his eyes, senses the cold-blooded killer inching its way towards him, its tongue flicking the air, tasting his body heat, and moving closer.

Holmes does nothing.

He continues to keep his eyes shut and as he does, he begins to drift away.

The darkness in his mind clears and he sees a young woman seated before him. She smiles into his face.

"Do you believe in miracles?"

"I do," Holmes replies.

"Do you believe in death?"

"I do not. We are each a Divine Spark of the Creator, the Light that shines within us all."

"Do you fear death?"

"No. Because it is only another form of change that this planet is dressed in. Hot cold. Light dark. Happy Sad. Life. Death. The Creator uses them to teach us."

The young woman smiles. "Your Master must be very proud of you."

Holmes smiled at her. "And other times he is not. But I continue to learn. That is all that matters."

She rises from before him, walks over and kisses him on the forehead. "We will meet again one day."

Sherlock smiles. "I pray it is soon."

She laughs.

Vanishes.

Holmes awakens from the vision to something cold snuggling in his lap.

He opens his eyes slowly. The cobra is now resting in his lap, eyes shut, soaking up his warmth.

Holmes smiles. Does not move.

He shuts his eyes to meditate again.

When he opens them again, the cobra is gone, and the Monk sits next to him.

"What did you learn, Sherlock?"

"That even death needs a time to rest."

The Monk laughed. "Not the lesson, young Sherlock, but for now, it will do."

He rises. Gestures'. "Come, it's almost dinner time."

Side by side, Sherlock and the Monk return to the ashram, neither talking, just enjoying the walk and sounds of nature about them.

KNIGHT MONT CASTLE

Sooth Berry Landing,

South London

Later

Sir Duvall Langersmith strutted back and forth in front of the large door to the so-called castle, impatient and irritated. If he had been a wild dog that moment, he might even have been frothing at the mouth. Which would have ruined the expensively coiffed beard and mustache he wore, as well as the quite expensive silk suit he wore.

Unable to pace any longer, he grunted angrily, then strode forth to grab a huge brass knocker on the door with the face of a gargoyle with wings.

The gargoyles eyes opened up and a stream of yellow light flooded out.

The illumination blinded Sir Duvall Langersmith a moment, then it vanished, the gargoyle was merely metal once more.

"Drat you! I shall have your head if you do not open this door at once!" Sir Duvall Langersmith hollered.

Silence.

Sir Duvall Langersmith banged the gargoyle's head repeatedly against the huge oak door, which responded with soft thuds. The wood was reinforced with steel in its frame, and it would take nothing less than a battering ram to break it down or make a dent.

Sir Duvall Langersmith banged the gargoyle's head one last time against the dense wood door, then shouted, "Come out, I know you're in there!"

The door made a loud, complaining sound as if it were being tortured or rudely awoken from a very deep sleep, and opened wide enough to show a familiar face.

"About time!" Sir Duvall Langersmith growled, then squeezed past the edge of the open door inside. The door shut behind him.

LABORATORY

Sir Duvall Langersmith paced the stone floor of the lab, hands behind his back, but temper brightly knit upon his frown and glaring eyes. "I have had enough of this. We must stop before it all gets out of hand."

The man who let him in, tugged the white smock he had been wearing from his shoulders and tossed it at the foot of a large cylinder inside which floated a naked body, devoid of any face or sexual indication.

He turned about to glare at Sir Duvall Langersmith, his eyebrows knit in their usual formidable, but annoying style. "I find your lack of faith in me most disturbing, Sir Duvall Langersmith."

"Then I suggest you reconsider our partnership, General Ogre," Sir Duvall Langersmith replied with hot arrows or despite flaming from his aged lips.

General Ogre frowned. "We've come too far to stop now."

Sir Duvall Langersmith strode forth and stabbed General Ogre hard on his chest. "You realize that the Queen now has Sherlock Holmes on the case."

"I do. And he will get nowhere with this. Our plan is too perfect."

"You mean your plan, do you not. It is not I who intends to overthrow the Queen and rise to the throne."

General Ogre grunted disapproval, his eyes narrowing in anger. "Do not threaten me!"

"I do not...threaten you. I am merely stating the facts!"

221B BAKER STREET

Ms. Hudson ushers into the sitting room Constable Evans, who is helping her carry four large silver trays. The ones the Constable Evans carries are laden with silverware, plates and huge pots of tea and coffee.

Her trays, which she has stacked in layers, overlapping each other, are loaded with scones, butter, fresh honey, rye, and wheat breads freshly baked, napkins and thinly sliced portions of beef and chicken.

They set the trays down on the table and Watson, and Conan rise to help serve and set the table.

Holmes watches with amusement as Watson tries desperately to keep Harry and Challenger's hands off the scones while he also sets the silverware about the table.

Finally, Watson grunts in disgust, and gives up, settling to have his fair share of the scones, then sit down next to Ms. Hudson who gives Holmes a wink and a nod.

Holmes rises from the fireplace where his reading chair is placed, lays down a book labeled, "Ancient Druid Tales of London," then joins everyone.

Harry passes rises and serves tea to everyone, while Watson and Ms. Hudson exchange quiet endearments. Finished, he sits next to Conan and smiles. "The feast of kings, is it not?"

Conan nods his head. His mouth is full of scone.

Watson glares at Conan a moment, then sighs. "Shall I never again have them all to myself, dear Ms. Hudson."

She leans close and whispers into his right ear. "I have saved half a tray for us...for later."

His eyes widen. "Us?"

She giggles, then leans into him. "Unless you're too tired..."

Watson quickly recovers his senses. "I am never too tired!" He responds a touch too loudly.

Everyone stops chatting and turns to look at him.

Harry teases. "Neither am I, dear Watson. Mina and I always have time."

Watson sinks deeply into his chair, face reddening with embarrassment.

Harry turns his attention...mercifully...away from Watson and nods to Homes. "Why, by the way, are we celebrating now? The case is not solved yet, is it?"

Holmes takes out a pocket watch and flips its cover to reveal the time. "No, but in another ten minutes it shall be."

KNIGHT MONT CASTLE

Sooth Berry Landing,

South London

Ten Minutes Later

After much banging on the door, it opens to reveal a quite distressed Sir Duvall Langersmith, wearing a night gown.

"Yes. Yes. What is this about that you disturb an old man's rest this time of evening?"

Inspector Bloodstone steps forward in front of Sergeant Price, who taps his nightstick warningly against the palm of his left hand. "I would speak with a bit more respect, were I you, Sir Duvall Langersmith."

Sir Duvall Langersmith ignores Sergeant Price. "Well?" He demands of Inspector Bloodstone.

Inspector Bloodstone smiles, his face resembling more like that of a wolf about to attack its victim, than a man about to speak. "I think you know quite well, why we are here, Sir Duvall Langersmith!"

Before Sir Duvall Langersmith can complain further or comment, the sound of a loud, but familiar voice is heard to speak, nearing from the right side of the front entrance.

Inspector Bloodstone turns to smile at his son, Constable Evans, as he pushes firmly, forward, General Ogre, followed by two other constables, with nightsticks at the ready.

Sir Duvall Langersmith glares at General Ogre at once. "I told you it was time to end this!"

"Shut up, you fool! They know nothing!"

General Ogre turns to Inspector Bloodstone, "I am sure Good Queen Mary will speak kindly of us, since we acted upon her orders."

Inspector Bloodstone's eyebrows soared upwards. "This shall be interesting to hear."

A constable came running up, with a small object in his right hand. He held it up for the Inspector to see. "An exact duplicate, Inspector."

It is the Spector caster device that Holmes showed the Inspector earlier.

Inspector Bloodstone smiled, revealing a nasty grin as he turned to General Ogre and Sir Duvall Langersmith who was now pale as a ghost.

"I suppose the Queen also asked you to use this to murder, Lady Henrietta?"

General Ogre and Sir Duvall Langersmith slumped in defeat.

Inspector Bloodstone turned to his son, Constable Evans. "Take these two away and lock them up!"

Constable Evans took the device from the constable to hand to the Inspector.

Inspector Bloodstone backed away. "This is one weapon I have no desire whatsoever to touch!"

221B BAKER STREET

Sitting Room

Later

A banging on the front door.

"I'll get it!" Harry speaks, then rushes downstairs to open up the door.

Sir Duvall Langersmith stands there alongside inspector Bloodstone and Constable Evans.

Harry grins. "Please do come in."

The three men enter and climb the stairs to the sitting room.

Harry shuts the front door and follows the three men upstairs.

Watson turns to look as the three enter.

"And now, we can finally celebrate now that Holmes is here.'

"Whatever do you mean, Harry and who is this stranger you have brought into our home?" Watson demands.

He turns to Holmes, who stays seated. "Did you invite them too?"

"I most certainly did," Sir Duvall Langersmith replies.

Watson jerks his head about in surprise as Sir Duvall Langersmith begins to peel off his hair, then his mustache then his nose, ears, and wrinkles from his face. He finally stands taller, revealing his handsome, but rugged face. "I most certainly did."

Watson turns to the Holmes seated next him. "Then who are you?"

The duplicate Holmes smiles but does not reply. Harry raises his right hand and the duplicate Holmes dissolves into a flowing swirl of light particles that slowly fade away.

Holmes sits down where his duplicate once was and smiles at his shocked friend. "Please forgive me, Watson, but this was a necessary trick to play."

"But we are all friends here," Conan pointed out.

"Yes, but..."

Holmes went to the windows overlooking Baker Street and swept the curtains aside. "If you please, gentleman."

Everyone rises to look out over Baker Street.

BAKER STREET

A struggling man is led away from the nearest alley to a police wagon by several constables.

221B BAKER STREET

Sitting Room

Later

Holmes turns to his friends. "I had to be sure that Sir Duvall Langersmith was not aroused by my suspicions. Otherwise, I could not have tricked General Ogre into revealing the truth."

"And now, if you do not mind, I would like to cleanse the grease paint from my face and change my clothes."

He smiles at Ms. Hudson. "I suspect you have a wonderful meal waiting for me."

Watson turns to Ms. Hudson, "You knew?"

Ms. Hudson smiles, gets up. Heads for the stairs. "I knew. Now to fetch dinner. Kept it warm for you, Sherlock."

Watson looks around at his friends. "You all knew!"

Harry shrugs. They would be watching you closely, Wasson. You have the kind of face that is hard to lie with.

221 B Baker Street

Sitting Room

Later

Holmes is seated in his favorite chair by the fireplace but turned towards his friends, scattered about the room. "And so, you see, once Harry, Challenger, and dear Conan here had discovered what I needed to know…"

Holmes holds up the small device with the odd wiring for everyone to see.

"Once I had that information complete, I knew what my next step had to be."

"And that is?"

"It's a bit of technology that Edison was playing with at one time, hoping to use it to bring some happiness to those who have lost a loved one."

"The General twisted it a bit."

"Yes, Watson. He did. Horribly so."

"How does it work?"

Holmes adjusted a control on the front of the box and a shape began to form in front of Watson.

Watson leaped to his feet. "My God! It summons ghosts!"

Holmes turned the adjustment off, and the shape vanished.

"Quite the contrary. According to Edison, it is nothing more than a simple projector which once programmed..."

"Programmed?" Challenger asked.

"It's the future of electronics according to Jules and Wells."

"You spoke to them as well?

"I did."

Watson frowned. "Very well. That is all well and good, but why would two such respected men agree to such a futile partnership in the first place?"

"The same reason all want to be dictators vie for position against the natural order of a society...to gain further power and influence for their narcissistic personalities."

Holmes paused a moment. But in this case, for Duvall, it was his ability to get rid of an annoyance to him."

"His wife?"

"Yes, Watson. Sad, but true. Some persons cannot live happily as long as their ex-partner lives.

"But how did you know it was them behind the murders?"

"Quite simple. Lady Henrietta was once married to Sir Duvall Langersmith, and therefore knew both his ambitions

and his ties to the cult of Spector."

"And?" Inspector Bloodstone asked. "What about the mysterious woman who supposedly murdered the victims?"

"Simulacrums."

Holmes set the device down on a side table then took his cold cup of coffee for a sip. Finished, he set it back down then smiled at Constable Evans. "Once I was admitted to General Ogre's residence and having fooled him with the help of Harry here and a bit of theatrical makeup, the General provided me with the rest of the help I needed to solve the case."

"But you had the Inspector and his men with you," Watson protested. "You might have been found out."

"I was not, was I? And my outfit more than fooled the unsuspecting, General."

Inspector Bloodstone chuckled. "That crusty old blaggart was so full of arrogance that he didn't suspect for a moment or believe that his plot had failed him."

"But what I don't understand," Conan spoke up. "Are why the simulacrums." He froze a moment then his face lit up. "But of course, to replace our Good Queen Mary and anyone else who might get in the way of their power grab."

Holmes smiled. "Excellent deduction, Conan."

Conan grinned. "It very well should be. After all, I did write you into existence."

Holmes smiled, "Perhaps I wrote you into existence, Conan. The multiverse we all live in is not restricted to just one version of us."

Conan gave Holmes a shocked look but did not protest. "Perhaps indeed."

Everyone broke into small chats about Conan and soon forgot about the murder case. Friendship is far more interesting than a string of cruel murders.

Watson and Ms. Hudson retreated from the room.

Harry began doing magic tricks.

Constable Evans and Inspector Bloodstone chatted amiably with Professor Challenger and Conan.

Holmes, no longer the center of attention, let his mind drift away to an earlier time in his life.

221B BAKER STREET

Sitting Room

Later

Holmes opens his eyes and smiles as he glances about the room at all his good friends. Inside his mind, he repeats what he just remembered…to himself. "Fear attracts fear, but love attracts love."

Watson pulls a chair next to Holmes and sits down. "Holmes, still one part of the case that mystifies me."

"Yes?"

"If General Ogre did not truly die, then who was the man I autopsied?"

"It seems the General was living a dual life, dear Watson."

"Meaning?"

"Literally. It is why he was able to operate so well in the Queen's service. There were two of him"

"Two? He had a doppelganger?"

Holmes chuckle. "No, Watson, he had a twin brother."

"Oh."

Holmes smiles at Watson, who shrugs. "Strange days never cease with us."

"No, they do not which brings me to the equalizer."

"Equalizer?"

Smiling Holmes rises and goes to the cabinet next to the sitting room table. He brings out the chess box, sets it down on the table and begins taking out the chess board and players.

The room goes suddenly quiet.

"Chess anyone?"

Challenger shakes his head. "I'm too tired to lose."

Conan rises to join Holmes. "I'm not!"

Challenger barks with laughter. "You never even come close to winning, Conan"

Conan sits down opposite Holmes. "Not yet I haven't, but if you give up, you never win."

Everyone breaks into laughter, then applauds.

Harry and Constable Evans join Holmes and Conan at the table. Holmes nods to Conan. "Take the first move, dear Conan."

Conan smiles. "Will. He moves his knight from behind his pawns into the front of them.

Challenger roars with laughter. "You'll never win by throwing your knight away, Conan."

Conan smiles. "Maybe."

AUTHOR'S NOTE

I have always had a great love for mystery and adventure. Starting with Agatha Christie's The Bat and ranging to Edgar Rice Burroughs Tarzan of the Apes and Jules Verne's Journey to the Center of the Earth.

It was only a short step between those three writers to run into Sir Arthur Conan Doyle and his wonderful Professor Challenger adventures.

I first read Sir Arthur Conan Doyle's wonderful spread of detective stories when I was still a child. I did not own books, so I read them at the public library, or at my school library. There was no Internet of Things, no Internet at all at the time. I was very into books as a child, always a loner of sorts. Even though I loved people, I was somehow always more in love with books. Call me bookworm then. Now bookworm writer. Maybe.

I went through the entire adult library in my hometown as a child, reading everything from fiction to non-fiction, science fiction to fantasy, and classic literature to modern. It did not matter. It was words on paper. I loved the smell of books. Still do, even though I cater to electronic books currently.

This is all a back-story of sorts to give you an idea of why my Sherlock Holmes while based somewhat on the canon of Doyle, are nevertheless much more than that. What would be the point of repeating what has already been done?

No, rather I saw this writing experience as an opportunity to allow my imagination to romp in his playground but take elements from other famous authors and stories I've loved over the years.

Obviously, there are copyright issues when it comes to living authors, so even though I would love to play in their yards too, that is forbidden territory. So, I have contented myself to take my love of classic literature...Doyle, Verne, Wells, Dumas, Shakespeare and pour them into a mutual melting pot. Kind of a United States of Literature, so to speak.

Whereas the Sherlock Holmes of Sir Arthur Conan Doyle functions out of London, England in the Victorian period; mine exists in a parallel world where all the authors who have ever lived and all their characters are alive at the same time.

Therefore, if you see me including Houdini and Sherlock together, Challenger and Conan Doyle, it makes more sense if they were alive on that world and not this one.

As a person of with a strong scientific background...I wrote a treatise on reaching other dimensions (parallel worlds) as an eighth grader, which my Physics teacher was knocked out about...I believe quite strongly in an unlimited universe, where an infinite number of parallel ones/dimensions exist at the same time.

When I was in India, I found that some there adhere to the belief that everything that man can do or imagine exists in a vast cosmic tapestry so that we do not so much physically exist, as mentally/spiritually move through that infinite tapestry, each choice we make...right or wrong...creating a branching point that we must follow, even though there were already an infinite number of other ones. Close to the parallel world/alternate dimension approach that many scientists are now coming to accept as a reality.

When I was a kid, the scientists barely believed in four dimensions...length, breadth, height, and time. Now as an adult there is talk of at least nine known dimensions.

But getting back to my stories, what makes them relevant and different is that I can populate them with any science, any character, any famous figure, writer, artist or whatever and they all fit! They fit because I created them. For fun. For pleasure. To be able to play on a field of dreams with no end in sight.

So, as you read my stories, dear reader, keep in mind that the Tesla car in my story is not Elon Musk's electric car, but a vehicle invented by collaboration between Thomas Edison and Nicolas Tesla in my invented world. It runs not by electricity as we know it, but by a different energy discovered by Tesla.

In my world Sherlock Holmes is not the first one of the stories, but one of several. Watson, likewise. Just as Spock was duplicated in the Star Trek series of movies to continue their worthy stories, so have I decided to include devices that will stimulate our imagination, take us to places we could never have gone before, and allow me to interject from time to time some of the wonderful insights I have been honored to receive as a maturing adult. So, death exists in my creation, but it has many permutations and outcomes. All exciting and mysterious.

Following this is a description of major characters, as well as items used exclusively in my Baker Street adventures.

GLOSSARY OF THE BAKER STREET UNIVERSE

A list of players, places and things that take place in the Baker Street Universe created by this author as the playground for his fantasies...and hopefully your own as well.

Bollocks...A common word used by the British to indicate something was nonsense, trash. An expletive.

Drat, dratted...A swear word like damn to indicate frustration.

Tosh...Sheer nonsense and an unkind reference to the upper class at that time.

Tesla Car...Device built by Ford in collaboration with Nicolas Tesla. Powered by a new form of energy unknown to our world yet.

Tesla devices...created by the team of Henry Ford, Thomas Edison, and Nicolas Tesla. Anything from lamps to frigs, to cooking devices. You name it; they have probably invented it in my world.

Moriarty...one of many. Professor Moriarty lives on in many and various manifestations for the sake of conflict, as well as invention and discourse. Where would a great detective be without a great villain to oppose him? While I do not feature Moriarty all the time, be warned he lurks behind the scenes! A lot!

Sherlock Holmes...Young man in his early twenties, comes from a humble home and a good upbringing. Precocious with a perfect memory. Not the cold fish of the Doyle series. Much kinder and humorous. Still with many of the same characteristics, but softened with a gentler personality, without losing the edges that give him an engaging purpose and deductions that are utterly amazing at times.

Watson, Doctor John...hero of the China Wars. Lost first love in China. Now in love with Mrs. Hudson. Loves Holmes like a brother. Doctor. Never without his black bag in which he carries his medical supplies and forensics tools that he and Sherlock often use in their investigations. Stocky with a bit of a stomach because of his love of scones, which I constantly use as a play of humor about the man.

Mrs. Hudson...not just a landlady anymore, but an integral part of the detective team...supplying support, as well as emotional and sometimes physical support. The glue that binds Watson and Holmes together. Again, in her twenties like Watson and Holmes. Lovely, but not beautiful, except of spirit. Kind and resourceful. Very shrewd and intelligent.

Lady Shareen...Lord Graystone's companion. A beautiful woman with a huge heart. She is responsible for helping women achieve social and financial equality. She also works to uplift the poor and homeless.

Professor Langston...the Invisible Man...a well-meaning doctor, who concocted a cocktail of chemicals that has forever altered his atomic structure such that he can turn invisible at will, though during emotional times of stress he can lose control of his visibility.

Inspector Bloodstone...a cantankerous policeman who has raving red hair, and a temper to match at times. Works with Holmes a lot but prefers to work on his own. Distrusts some of the intuitive moments of Holmes, but overall will go with what he reveals as Holmes is more often right than wrong in his deductions.

Constable Evans...the long-lost son of Inspector Bloodstone. Also red haired, like his father, but with no temper and a great personality. Everyone likes him.

Queen Mary of Scots...has never existed. Instead, this one is a derivation of Mary, who was beheaded and Victoria. Much more intelligent, progressive, but a leader in every sense of the word.

Magic...exists in this world of Sherlock as does science. Both are equally as relevant to the action and scenery of the stories.

Fairie...a land that exists in parallel to Sherlock's world and through which Lord Graystone (Lord of the Jungle) came through to become part of the Baker Street Brotherhood.

Fairie is richly endowed with magical creatures and monsters, Elves, fairies, and other fun things, as well as endless realms of green Amazon like lands. Dragons. Which have played a part in several of my first stories and a few later ones.

Nicolas Tesla...a genius who has dedicated his life to upgrading the quality of life for everyone on the planet. Witty, charming, and dangerous.

Harry Houdini...swarthy, suave, into magic in every way...physical and the real thing.

Professor Challenger...very tall, built like a bear, flaming red beard and hair. Quick to temper, but a kind man with a great mind. An adventurer beyond measure.

Captain Nemo...a reformed pirate with a mind that grasps mechanics that rivals Henry Ford and Nicolas Tesla. Is famous for his extremely powerful weapon of the sea...the Nautilus.

Jules Verne...a genius when it comes to theories and fiction, blonde, extremely friendly, caring, and adventurous. Teams up often with H.G. Wells, a friend he grew up with. Designer of the Master of the World, which in another set of Victorian adventures he uses to fight an invasion from Mars.

H.G. Wells...a brilliant writer and navigator. Contributes to the flying device Master of the World and its ability to fly through space and time. Very British and a bit stuffy at times.

Alexander Dumas...a French friend of Jules in one of the worlds I have created for Jules to explore in unique adventures that do not include H.G. Wells. Huge man with a lust for adventure and fighting.

Henry Ford...still an arrogant man, but more willing to help others, and often teams up with Tesla to do projects. Not prominent yet in my stories but working on it.

Master of the World...a huge flying machine that resembles a cross between a dirigible and a submarine that travels utilizing String theory, with an engine that converts string energy into fuel that can thrust the ship between parallel worlds, as well as back and forth in time. Created by Jules Verne, but later improved by H.G. Wells after their battle with the Martians detailed in my prior series starting with Invaders.

Lord Graystone...my version of Tarzan, but instead of being raised by apes, he was raised by a bull dragon. Highly educated and a loyal supporter of Queen Mary of Scots and husband of Lady Shareen. Sponsors numerous charities for the poor and unwanted. Champion of Fairie.

Hyde...Doctor Jekyll performs an experiment on himself that separates the evil portion of him into a unique entity. This entity is pure evil and pure energy. It can possess anyone and once having done so, become that person. Cause them to do the unthinkable to achieve its evil plans.

Doctor Jekyll...a kind, young teacher who has made a horrible miscalculation and created an abomination of himself.... Hyde! A creature that is pure evil.

Dracula...not the Bran Stoker version, but my own. Misunderstood, not eternal and drinking human blood when no other choice is possible.

Conan Doyle...the dead Sir Arthur Conan Doyle brought from our world to the alternate reality which he is reborn into, healthy and young once more. Also, an integral part of the great detective's team at times.

Baker Street Brotherhood...a team of operatives who, upon occasion, help Sherlock and Watson in their missions. Some of the more notable ones are Lord Graystone (Lord of the Jungle), Madame Curie, Dracula, Professor Langston (The Invisible Man), Professor Challenger (also a Conan Doyle character), Sir Arthur Conan Doyle himself (reborn from our world to the new one without losing awareness of himself), Lady Shareen (our equivalent of Indiana Jones), Jules Verne and H.G. Wells.

Obviously, there are many, many more, but these are the most frequently guested characters in my stories and novels.

REQUEST FOR REVIEW

If you found some pleasure in reading my work, please take the time to leave a review for it. Authors can thrive or die for the lack of reviews.

Thanking you in advance for your kindness.

John